GEO

3/00

The Magic Hill

A. A. MILNE

The Magic Hill

illustrated by Isabel Bodor Brown

DUTTON CHILDREN'S BOOKS ❦ NEW YORK

For Stuart, Sarah, Emily, and Betsy
I. B. B.

Text copyright © 1925 by A. A. Milne

Illustrations copyright © 2000 by Isabel Bodor Brown

Published by arrangement with Lesley Milne

All rights reserved.

CIP Data is available.

Published in the United States 2000 by Dutton Children's Books.

a division of Penguin Putnam Books for Young Readers

345 Hudson Street, New York, New York 10014

http://www.penguinputnam.com/yreaders/index.htm

Designed by Ellen M. Lucaire

Printed in Hong Kong ● First Edition

ISBN 0-525-46147-7

1 3 5 7 9 10 8 6 4 2

The Magic Hill

When I was a little girl, my mother read me this story from an old book that her mother had read to *her* when she was little. The pictures were missing, so I made up my own inside my head. That copy of the book somehow got lost, but the story and my pictures remained in my head for many years until I told it to my own daughters.

Finally I decided that such a charming story should be told again, and that I'd put those pictures that were in my head onto paper. I hope they are worthy of Mr. Milne.

—Isabel Bodor Brown

nce upon a time there was a king who
had seven children. The first three were boys, and
he was glad about this, because a King likes to
have three sons. But when the next three were
boys also, he was not so glad, and he wished that
one of them had been a daughter.

So the Queen said, "The next shall be a daughter." And it was, and they decided to call her Daffodil.

When the Princess Daffodil was a month old, the King and Queen decided to give a great party in the Palace for the christening. The Fairy Mum-ruffin was invited to be Godmother to the little Princess.

"She is a good fairy," said the King to the Queen, "and I hope she will give Daffodil something that will be useful to her. Beauty or Wisdom or Riches or—"

"Or Goodness," said the Queen.

"Or Goodness, as I was about to remark," said the King.

So you will understand how anxious they were when Fairy Mumruffin looked down at the sleeping Princess in her cradle and waved her wand.

"They have called you Daffodil," she said, and then she waved her wand again.

Let Daffodil
The gardens fill.
Wherever you go,
Flowers shall grow.

There was a moment of silence while the King tried to think this out.

"What was that?" he whispered to the Queen. "I didn't quite get that."

"Wherever she walks, flowers are going to grow," said the Queen. "I think it's sweet."

"Oh," said the King. "Was that all? She didn't say anything about—"

"No."

"Oh, well."

He turned to thank Fairy Mumruffin, but she had already flown away.

It was nearly a year later that the Princess first began to walk, and by this time everybody had forgotten about the Fairy's promise. So, when he came back from hunting one day, the King was rather surprised to find his favorite courtyard, where he used to walk when he was thinking, dotted with flowers.

"What does this mean?" he said sternly to his chief gardener.

"I don't know, Your Majesty," said the gardener, scratching his head. "It isn't my doing."

"Then who has done it? Who has been here today?"

"Nobody, Your Majesty, except Her Royal Highness Princess Daffodil, as I've been told, though how she found her way here, such a baby and all, bless her sweet little—"

"That will do," said the King. "You may go." For now he remembered. This was what the Fairy Mumruffin had promised.

That evening the King and the Queen talked the matter over very seriously before they went to bed.

"It is quite clear," said the King, "that we cannot let Daffodil run about everywhere. That would never do. She must take her walks on the flower beds. She must be carried across all the paths. It will be annoying in a way, but in a way, it will be useful. We shall be able to do without most of the gardeners."

"Yes, dear," said the Queen.

So Daffodil as she grew up was only allowed
to walk on the beds, and the other children were
very jealous of her because they were only allowed
to walk on the paths; and they thought what fun
it would be if only they were allowed to run about
on the beds just once.

But Daffodil thought what fun it would be
if she could run about on the paths like the other
boys and girls.

One day, when the Princess was about five years old, a Court Doctor came to see her. And after he looked at her tongue, he said to the Queen: "Her Royal Highness needs more exercise. She must run about more. She must climb hills and roll down them. She must hop and skip and jump. In short, Your Majesty, although she is a Princess, she must do what other little girls do."

"Unfortunately," said the Queen, "she is not like other little girls." And she sighed and looked out the window. And out of the window, at the far end of the garden, she saw a little green hill where no flowers grew. So she turned back to the Court Doctor and said, "You are right; she must be as other little girls."

So she went to the King, and the King gave Princess Daffodil the little green hill for her very own. And every day the Princess played there, and flowers grew; and every evening the girls and boys of the countryside came and picked the flowers.

So they called it the Magic Hill. And, from that day onward, flowers have always grown on the Magic Hill, and boys and girls have laughed and played and picked them.

The End